The Magic Porridge Pot

A Viking Easy-to-Read Classic

retold by **Harriet Ziefert**
illustrated by **Emily Bolam**

VIKING

VIKING
Published by the Penguin Group
Penguin Books USA Inc., 375 Hudson Street, New York, New York 10014, U.S.A.
Penguin Books Ltd, 27 Wrights Lane, London W8 5TZ, England
Penguin Books Australia Ltd, Ringwood, Victoria, Australia
Penguin Books Canada Ltd, 10 Alcorn Avenue, Toronto, Ontario, Canada M4V 3B2
Penguin Books (N.Z.) Ltd, 182-190 Wairau Road, Auckland 10, New Zealand

Penguin Books Ltd, Registered Offices: Harmondsworth, Middlesex, England

First published in 1997 by Viking, a division of Penguin Books USA Inc.
Published simultaneously in Puffin Books

1   3   5   7   9   10   8   6   4   2

ISBN 0-670-86811-6

Printed in U.S.A.
Set in Bookman

Viking® and Easy-to-Read® are registered trademarks of Penguin Books USA Inc.

Reading Level 1.6

The Magic Porridge Pot

There once was a little girl
who lived with her mother.
They were poor and had
no money for food.

One day, the mother said,
"All I have for you
is one small cracker.
Make it last."

The little girl went out to play.
Along came an old man.
"Can you give me something to eat?"
he asked.

"Yes," said the little girl.
She gave him her cracker.

"Thank you," said the old man.
"And here is a present for you.

"This is a magic pot.
When you want to eat, say,
'Little pot, cook!'
When you have eaten all you want,
say, 'Little pot, stop!'"

The little girl ran home.

She put the pot on the table.
She said, "Little pot, cook!"
The pot began to fill
with porridge.

The little girl ate two bowls
of porridge.
Her mother ate two bowls.
They were full and happy.

Then the little girl said,
"Little pot, stop!"
The pot stopped making porridge.

One day, the little girl
went out to play.
Her mother wanted some porridge.
"I don't need to call my little girl,"
she said. "I know what to do."

She looked at the pot and
said, "Cook, little pot."

Nothing happened.

So she said, "Little pot, cook!"
And the little pot began
to fill with porridge.

The mother ate a bowlful.
While she ate, the pot
was filling itself up again.

"No more, little pot!"
said the mother.

The pot went on filling.

"Little pot, no more,"
said the mother.

And the pot went on filling.

Porridge began to run over
the top of the pot.
"Little pot, don't cook!"
said the mother.

Porridge poured out of the pot,
over the table,
and onto the floor.
"Don't cook, little pot!"

"Oh dear, oh my!
  What are the right words?
  What should I say?"
asked the mother.

Faster and faster came the porridge.
Up the walls . . .
out the door . . .

. . . and down the street!

"No, no, porridge pot!"
the mother said.

But nothing stopped the porridge.

The little girl saw a river of
porridge coming toward her.

She guessed what had happened.

She shouted, "Little pot, stop!"

The pot heard her and stopped.

Everyone brought spoons.
They ate and ate
until they got back home.

DATE			